The Monster in the Moat

and other
short stories

**selected by
Stewart Ross**

Illustrations by Ellie Davies, Age 10, Eckington Junior School, Derbyshire; Flo Balmer and Mary Sacker, Age 8, Ipswich High Junior School; Lauren Docherty, Age 11, Garrowhill Primary School, Glasgow.

The Monster in the Moat

and other
short stories

An anthology of winning stories from the 2008-2009
World Book Day Short Story competition

In association

NATE

Published in 2009 by Evans Brothers Limited
2A Portman Mansions
Chiltern Street
London W1U 6NR

British Library Cataloguing in Publication Data
A catalogue record for this book is available from the British Library

ISBN: 9780237538224

Editor: Bryony Jones
Designers: Rebecca Fox, Evans
Jo Kennedy, Us2Design

Foreword

I find it difficult to believe what I have been
reading. These stories are by primary school
children? Impossible! Many of them are better
than adult equivalents published in magazines.
Anyone wanting to know what the young are
thinking nowadays, how their minds are working,
is urged to read this terrific collection – and
stand amazed at its skill, inventiveness, vitality,
sensitivity and wit. I am honoured, truly, to have
been asked to make the selection.

Mind you, it was an almost impossible task…
There were at least ten moat monster tales worthy
of inclusion, for instance. So, if your story is not
here, please remember that this is not a collection
of *the* best stories – although they are all excellent
– but a selection *from* the best fifty or so. Our aim
has been to produce a broad cross-section of the
finest modern children's writing, representing all
regions, ages and styles. As a result, and because
we are limited to just ten examples, we have had
to leave many splendid pieces of writing on one
side. That said, there was one we just could not
bring ourselves to omit because it was so original
and amusing: nine-year-old Rhys Pearson-Shaul's
delightful moat monster story – in verse! It's

included as a bonus.

In making our final selection we did come across a number of the stories that were sadly over-written, full of convoluted sentences and clogged with superfluous adjectives. In a bid to fight against this, I link arms with George Orwell. In 'Politics and the English Language' (1946) this master of modern prose suggested: 'Never use a long word where a short one will do' and 'If it is possible to cut a word out, always cut it out.' Although Orwell was not talking about what he called 'the literary use of language', his advice holds pretty good for most of us attempting to communicate effectively with our fellow human beings – especially if we bear in mind his last rule: 'Break any of these rules sooner than say anything outright barbarous'!

Two aspects of the best stories astonished me. One was the degree of intellectual and emotional maturity they showed (look at Theodore Ross' moat story, for instance); the other was the sophisticated way several authors played with the opening sentences they had been given. It was as if they had said to themselves, 'Hey, that's a pretty naff beginning. How can I turn it into something more interesting?' Hence Hugh Blayney's moat warmed by the Lakebed Heating Co.

Last year I singled out my favourite story. There are too many gems for that to be possible this time, but I would like to congratulate the Welsh, Irish and overseas schools for their delightful contributions. Once again, huge votes of thanks are due to the heroic teachers who continue to inspire, assist and instruct our young writers, and to World Book Day and the Evans Publishing Group for organising a remarkable venture. Together they have enabled this precious anthology of sparkling talent to appear. Above all, though, our thanks and congratulations must go to the young authors themselves. The future is bright indeed.

Stewart Ross
Blean, 2009

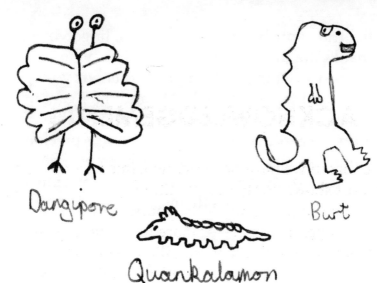

Dangipore

Burt

Quankalamon

Panticora

Penelopie

Frank-Firter.

Dacknish

ACKNOWLEDGEMENTS

Once again we have been overwhelmed by the support shown for the competition.

So thank you to all the young writers who have put pen to paper - or more likely, fingers to keyboards - and to the young illustrators who have sent us some delightful pictures. It has been a privilege for us to read and review your work.

Congratulations to our talented winners. And if you didn't win this year, keep at it – maybe next year will be your year!

Thank you too, to all the teachers, librarians and parents who encouraged our entrants to write so creatively for this competition.

Special thanks are also due to the authors who provided first lines, and to their publishers, with an honourable mention for Stewart Ross who has freely given so much of his time to read the shortlist of entries and write the foreword. His tireless enthusiasm for the art of writing and the importance of books for children is an inspiration to everyone.

Thank you also to Cathy Schofield of World Book Day, Kate Bostock of the Publishers Association, and Truda Spruyt and Chris Baker from Colman Getty for supporting the competition so wholeheartedly once more.

Log on to **www.worldbookday.com** or
www.evansbooks.co.uk for news of next year's
competition.

CONTENTS

Grump and the Credit Cruncher
Hugh Blayney   17

There was once a monster who lived
in a moat... Theodore Ross   21

The Monster in the Moat
(A story in verse) Rhys Pearson-Shaul   25

Tom and the Book Sophia Miller   31

Spider Boy Gemma Daubeney   37

Give them back! Orla Heatley   43

Rules Out! Emily Brown   49

A Brilliant Birthday Present Sam Wheeler   55

The Poisoned Juice Emma Kerslake   59

Maggie's Tale Ria Burke   65

Cuckoo Magic Emily James   69

There was once a monster who lived in a moat.

Julia Donaldson

Grump and the Credit Cruncher

by Hugh Blayney

There was once a monster who lived in a moat.
This is very impractical, since the Lakebed
Heating Co. charges so much money that even
Grump's treasure trove didn't last for long.
Grump lives at the bottom of a moat because he
doesn't want… urgh *humans* walking in on his
life. Grump, as you may have guessed, is the
monster that lives at the bottom of the moat.
He is about the size of a house with green fur
all over his vaguely human-shaped body. He
has bloodstained spines all down his back (it's
actually red food colouring, but you're not
supposed to know that) and red eyes. Everybody
hates him, much to his pleasure. We join him just
entering the office of Mr Cold, head of Lakebed
Heating Co.

'Oh no, not him again,' muttered Mr Cold
under his breath, then loudly he said, 'How may
I err… oh!' Mr Cold had forgotten just how *big*
Grump was. 'Err… oh yes, err… oh n-n-no, tell
me he hasn't remembered that change we were
meant to give him,' he muttered.

'NO, I HAVE COME TO SAY THAT I CAN'T PAY THE HEATING BILL,' Grump boomed.

A strange glint came to Mr Cold's eyes and he sneered, 'Too bad, I'll take your house instead.'

'NOOOOOOOOOOOOOOOOOO!' yelled Grump.

'You have a week to pay us £20,988,745, plus interest,' said Mr Cold.

Grump fainted.

Once the SAS had dragged Grump back next to his moat, he awoke in the middle of a frenzy of activity. People were shouting, 'It's the credit crunch! (Scream!)' and, 'The banks are disappearing with our money, too!'

Grump slowly realised that he could try to find this money, and pay off his debts! But life is never as simple as that, and this is no exception.

Back in his house Grump was researching, which is difficult when you are underwater. He had found out that his brother's nickname was Cruncher, which sounded like it might have a remote connection to The Credit Crunch, if there was any possibility that there was any connection at all. He had also found people called: Crump, Chill, Bill (I suppose this rhymes with chill) and Billiard (begins with bill, that rhymes with chill).

After days and days of research he had learnt one thing: that he was wasting his time, precious time that was about to be used to find out what was destroying the banks. Time to do something. Time was short, 40cm tall to be precise, and rapidly shrinking.

So four hours later, at 10.34 pm, Grump was hiding, watching the bank. He had until seven-thirty when it would start to get light again. Just then he heard an unearthly sound, like fingers scraping down a blackboard, only far worse.

'Murgh muggh murgh mu mu murgh mu murgh mu ma ma mu murgh murgh muggh murgh mu mu murgh mu murgh mu ma ma mu murgh.'

Then Grump heard it far more clearly and heard, sung in a very bad singing voice, 'I AM THE CREDIT CRUNCHER, I AM A MEAN MACHINE. I AM THE ULTIMATE LUNCHER, EATING ALL THE BANKS CLEAN, CRUNCH, LUNCH, CRUNCH, CRUNCH, CRUNCH.'

This was followed by a series of thuds, obviously footsteps. And then Grump saw him. He was at least two times the size of Grump, with vicious fighting claws, but he was very fat. To make up for this he was coated in coins, like armour. Grump realised that he could not beat him in fighting, he would have to be sneaky.

Then Grump looked at the monster's feet. They were not covered, instead they were shoes with weird wheels on the bottom. The thuds had been the brakes. The Credit Cruncher couldn't move on his own... and the brakes were only screwed on... and they were on a slope leading to a cliff into the sea... bingo!

It only took a few seconds to undo the

brakes, but no book could describe the chaos that followed, so I can barely scratch the surface when I say that the bank was flattened anyway, and the Credit Cruncher never resurfaced from the sea. But Grump took the money from the bank, and then lived a happy and rich life... until Mr Recession came... from America.

Hugh Blayney, age 10
The Hawthorns School, Surrey

There was once a monster who lived in a moat...

by Theodore Ross

'There was once a monster who lived in a moat...'
I copied down the opening sentence of our
English homework and carried on the story:

*'The moat surrounded a magical castle with a
high tower where a beautiful princess was imprisoned.
Every day she looked out across the land, waiting for
her knight in shining armour who would finally defeat
the evil moat monster and rescue her.'*

Yeah, yeah, I thought. *Blah-blah-blah.* I can give
Mr B. what he wants for prep. Fairytale castles
and damsels in distress are fine, but unless I can
come up with an English essay for Bruno the bully
by break time, my life is not going to be worth
living. Monsters in moats are one thing, but right
now I have real monsters of my own to deal with.
And mine was sitting behind me, flicking bits of
chewed-up paper at my back.

*'And so the valiant knight took off on his trusty
steed to a distant land to challenge the moat monster
and do battle.'*

I didn't need to turn around to know that Bruno was grinning at me from his desk. He was big and ugly and I could almost feel his stinky breath on the back of my neck. He was clutching his ruler in one hand, silently poking it into the other. He was my monster. No doubt about it. No moat required. He was going to get me, and I was scared. I thought about the knight's trusty steed and wondered if my bike was fast enough to get me as far as the park before Bruno caught up with me. Small beads of sweat started to appear on my forehead.

'Get on with it boy,' the teacher said as I glanced towards the door. 'I want these in before the end of the day.'

'The vicious monster clasped the knight in his ugly claws and began to squeeze his throat...' I wrote.

Bruno would like this. Last week he pinned me up against the toilet wall. I could still feel his sweaty hands around my neck. His eyes were mean and kind of mad. I spent my life trying to avoid him, darting into corners and doorways round school praying I wouldn't be seen. My heart was pounding faster at the thought of another beating. I was no hero. There were no knights in shining armour when I needed them.

'The knight drew out his magical sword and struck the monster, wounding its scaly chest.'

You hear about bullying on telly and that, but it's very different when it's happening to you. Bruno grinned horribly at me again from behind his textbook. He spat at me, made a kind of hissing sound and sniggered. This was for real. This was not some kind of fairy story. Bruno was going to kick my head in if I didn't get this essay to him and no one was going to come to my rescue. Every muscle in my body was tense. As Mr B. walked past my desk, I could hardly write.

'Are you finished yet?' he asked.

'Yes sir, nearly – not quite at the end,' I replied, glancing over my shoulder at Bruno who was cracking his knuckles and making menacing movements with his hands.

Whatever I wrote was going to be wrong. A couple more paragraphs and that was it. Bruno didn't need a reason. My eyes started to water. I could already feel my head throbbing, just like it had for days afterwards. You don't forget your first beating. I told my mum I fell over when she found my blazer ripped, but there was no way to hide the blood on my shirt. I still had the purple bruises on my arms and the cut inside my mouth. The lesson was almost over. Just a few more lines to go. There was no way to avoid him now.

'With a final lunge the brave knight stabbed the evil monster through the heart and it fell dead at his feet.'

The bell rang out in the hall. It was the end of the lesson. I could feel Bruno's big shape moving closer. I stopped writing. My blood was racing through me but my hand froze.

'Last few minutes,' the teacher announced.

'You should almost be at the end.'

I glanced over at Bruno. His grey eyes met mine and the corner of his mouth twitched. I recognised that sneer and I felt sick. I looked up at my teacher who was waiting impatiently. Time to finish. For a second, I longed for the world of fairytales and monsters in moats.

'And they all lived happily ever after,' I wrote.

Theodore Ross, age 9
New College School, Oxford

The Monster in the Moat
(A story in verse)
by Rhys Pearson-Shaul

There was once a monster who lived in a moat,
With the tail of a fish and the head of a goat,
He lived out his days in the cool of the moat,
And watched as people went by in a boat.

He had eight spiny legs and eyes which were yellow,
His tummy was fat like a giant marshmallow.
His roar was a squeak, no sign of a bellow,
He really felt sad, this lonely young fellow.

His face was all wrinkled like an old granny's skin,
His smile was enormous, a giant of a grin,
And his teeth that sparkled like a star at night,
Provided the moat with a source of bright light.

He lived underwater so not to be seen,
And his body could change from purple to green,
He ate a bold knight every now and then,
On a day he was hungry, he ate about ten.

His home was a cavern which hid in the rocks,
And had numerous windows with glistening locks,
The doors were all made of strong shiny steel,
With hinges all cast from an old fishing reel.

He sat and he wished for a change in his luck,
He was getting so tired of living in muck.
Many a time he had tried to break free,
But what held him back was what people might see.

He worried and worried until he was sick,
The answer was to plan an escape which was quick,
He thought long and hard of what he should do,
But all of his plans needed not one, but two.

Eventually he had the most brilliant thought,
A partner in crime is what must be sought.
He put out an advert in the Castle Express,
And waited and waited for one to impress.

One day as he sat on his favourite place,
Wishing and wondering for a castle with space,
As he dreamt of a future with small ones around,
A beautiful creature made a beautiful sound.

What was this creature who sang like a bird,
A voice which was special, the best he had heard?
He saw in the distance a figure appear
With a long swishing tail and long golden hair.

She swam right up to him and sang a sweet ditty,
His eyes were transfixed since she was so pretty.
She beckoned to him to follow her trail,
He realised at last that his dream could not fail.

She led him away to the bank at the edge,
Then she slipped out the water and sat on a ledge.
The monster he followed her out into the world,
And waited alongside her as his dream unfurled.

She gently kissed him and whispered a rhyme
Then life seemed to move in double-quick time.
His mind went all fuzzy and the next thing he knew,
In front of him stood a castle, brand new.

The monster had found a wife he could love,
And their marriage was sealed by the release of a dove.
They lived in a fine castle happily ever after,
With children galore it was filled with laughter.

Rhys Pearson-Shaul, age 9
Taverham Hall School, Norfolk

Alex had squashed many spiders in his time, but he never expected one to try and squash him back!

Steve Cole

Tom and the Book

by Sophia Miller

'Alex had squashed many spiders in his time, but he never expected one to try and squash him back!'
Tom put down the book and sighed. How ridiculous! He too, had squashed many spiders in his time, but as if one would even try to squash him back! He shook his head, and lay down on his bed to look up at the wooden ceiling of the chalet. It was homely and warm, and Tom felt as safe as houses wrapped up in the soft duvet of his cosy bed. He turned out the light, rolled on to his side, and fell straight into a peaceful sleep, the book still lying open on the bed.

When Tom awoke, something was different. He was not in his warm bed in the chalet, but on a hard, cold metal surface. You could hardly call that a bed! Now very worried, Tom slowly got out of bed, and finding that there were no clothes in the room, was forced to stay in his pyjamas, which looked faded and dirty. He tiptoed out of the room, and finally, after a fair bit of aimlessly wandering about the house, he came across the kitchen. As he seated himself at the table, the thought came to him that this house seemed very alike to the one in his book – the one about the boy called Alex who liked to squash spiders… He shook that thought out of his head.

Don't be ridiculous, Tom, he thought. *How could you be in the book anyway?*

Just as Tom was considering this, a strange woman walked into the room. Her feet were bony and thin; she was wearing no shoes or socks. Her legs were like matchsticks, yet hairy, and her knees were knobbly. She was wearing a raggedy dress and an apron splattered with the remains of last night's dinner. Her arms hung by her sides, her hands twitching mechanically. The sagging, yellow skin on her face was just as horrifying as her features – a wrinkled old mouth, pursed as if she was tasting a sour lemon, a warty crooked nose – and her eyes. Not eyes as such, they looked like the black buttons from his grandma's coat sewn on with dental floss. Tom was aghast. He'd never, ever seen anything like her in his life. The housekeeper perhaps?

'Hello, young man,' she smiled, showing her decaying yellow teeth. 'What's your name?'

'T-Tom,' stammered Tom. 'My name's Tom.'

The woman looked bemused. 'There's nobody named 'Tom' in this book,' she rasped, sounding almost angry.

Tom was now aware of the circumstances. He realised he had gone to sleep with the book lying over him, and he must have slipped into the story during the night… He knew he had to get back home before he got to the part where the huge spider attacked Alex…

'How do I get back home?' he asked the woman boldly. She smiled and shook her head.

'Now, now, my dear,' she tutted patronisingly. 'The only way to escape is to find The Book…' She shrugged.

So he set off to try and find the book. He bounded upstairs, on a mission. Soon he had managed to find Alex's room. It had a large sign with a skull on it saying: ALEX'S ROOM. PLEEZ ENTUR AT YOUR OWN RISC. Although Tom could understand what it said, he went in anyway. He saw a smelly, grubby little boy about his age sitting on the floor, scribbling on a piece of paper. He looked up at Tom.

'Oi you!' he shouted. 'Can't you read?'

'Yeah, your spelling and handwriting was really neat,' Tom replied sarcastically.

'Well good, then you should know that you should GET OUT!' answered the boy, obviously not getting Tom's remark.

Reluctantly, Tom shuffled outside and sat down next to Alex's door. After five minutes, Alex reappeared to stick another notice on his door, then stuck his tongue out at Tom and strode off. Tom stood up to read the notice. It said: IF YU ENTUR YOR DED. Tom smirked and ran off to follow Alex.

Tom found Alex in the garden. He knew only too well that Alex would soon be attacked by the giant spider – he had to hurry. Alex was squatting on the grass, watching over a spider. Tom had to distract him before he squashed it.

'Hey you!' he shouted.

Alex was not listening.

'I said, hey you!' repeated Tom.

Finally Alex turned around. 'What now?' he sighed. 'And who are you anyway?'

'I'm Tom,' said Tom. 'And I want to know where The Book is!'

'What book?' puzzled Alex.

Tom knew that he was a – let's say a simple-minded boy – and he didn't waste too much time thinking. Tom was getting impatient. So he spoke his mind. Big Mistake.

'You know,' chatted Tom, 'I have NEVER, EVER, met such an unintelligent person in my life before!'

Alex's face contorted into an expression of utter fury and contempt.

Oops! thought Tom, as he was chased around the garden. He looked over his shoulder at Alex. He was out of control! He was swinging mighty punches and kicks, occasionally hitting trees and wailing like a banshee. Tom had known Alex was a bit dim-witted, but he now looked like a champion boxer! He hadn't known that! Alex was getting nearer. Tom sprinted faster, the ground a blur beneath his feet.

CRASH! BOOF! Tom had tripped over an old television sitting at the back of the garden – don't ask me what it was doing there! Alex had seen the opportunity and slammed Tom in the face. Ouch!

Tom sat up, feeling a little worse for wear, but at least he was conscious. He looked up at the television he had tripped over. Miraculously, it had turned itself on! Tom sighed longingly as he saw his cosy little room back home on the screen! Then Tom remembered Alex. Oh no! He had squashed the spider, and just like in the book, the giant spider now had Alex in his clutches and was trying to squash him as Alex shrieked in pain. Tom then noticed The Book propped up against the television set! Without thinking, he snatched up The Book, raced towards Alex, pulled him free, then together they dived into the television screen.

It was only when they were sitting in Tom's room at home that it dawned on Tom that the giant spider had had big, black, button eyes…

Sophia Miller, age 11
St George's International School, Luxembourg

Spider Boy

by Gemma Daubeney

Alex had squashed many spiders in his time but he never expected one to try and squash him back! Alexander Thomas was a disgusting child who liked to do nothing other than squash innocent spiders, and this is why a terrible incident came about.

Alex was sitting in the old oak tree in his garden. It was a sunny day near the end of August. Alex had been sitting in this tree for several hours, ever since breakfast it seemed, doing his favourite thing… spider squashing!

It was a perfect day for spider squashing and the old oak tree was a perfect place to do it, so there Alex sat. He was just cornering a large spider when another crawled over his leg and bit his hand. He shook his throbbing hand and nearly fell out of the tree.

The spider bite didn't have any effect on Alex until he took off the plaster his mum had given him. When he removed it, he saw that the bite had turned a nasty shade of green! Alex looked at the spider bite in horror, he never expected any spiders in his neat garden to be poisonous. Alex decided not to tell his mum for she would only say that it served him right for squashing so many spiders.

Alex woke up the next morning to find himself in considerable pain and almost suffocating in stifling heat. He tried to lift the large weight from his body but found his arms weak and unable to move. Alex only felt fresh air when his mum came in and plucked the duvet off his bed and found no Alex – he was there but very tiny!

Alex stared at himself in horror, he could only see his arms and legs but they looked no longer than half a matchstick. He sat down on his huge mountain of a bed and thought, *If I can't jump down off the bed or be picked up and put on the floor, how can I get down?*

Suddenly Alex had a brainwave: he crawled all the way across his bed and slid down the bed post! Then he toddled across his untidy bedroom floor. Alex then walked into the kitchen to find his mum eating breakfast, his dad reading the newspaper and his sister plaiting her Barbie's hair. There was nothing strange about this except they all ignored Alex – it was as if he was something very small and nasty, a bit like a spider! Alex realised quite soon that he was going to get no breakfast, so he crept through the cat flap into the garden to do some more spider squashing.

'Aaaaaaaaaaaaaaaaaaaaaaaaaahhhhhhhhhh!'

screamed Alex as he looked into the laser-red eyes of a huge spider!

Then the Alex-sized spider spoke in a voice as deep as thunder, 'You are a repulsive little boy, Alexander William Thomas, and we spiders think you are evil. You have squashed many of my family members and for this I shall squash you back!'

Alex started running wildly around the garden in hope of escaping from the huge spider who was too quick for Alex. He realised his only escape was to quickly clamber up the old oak tree. Alex had just reached the top of the tree when the huge spider looked straight at him and started climbing the tall tree himself. The Alex-sized spider took a second compared to the amount of time Alex spent, and before he knew it the spider was advancing on him with his eight eyes rolling, his long and lanky legs twitching feverishly and his menacing fangs glinting in the morning sun.

'Alex, you have done no good in this world and have squashed one spider too many and now you shall die!' the Alex-sized spider declared.

'No, please don't kill me! I didn't mean to kill any spiders and I'll never squash another one ever, I promise!' Alex screamed loudly, almost crying.

'Are you sure you really won't hurt another of my fellows?' the giant spider questioned suspiciously.

'I'm sure, honest,' Alex replied pleadingly.

'Well then, I will change you back to human size,' the giant spider said smartly. Alex felt relief flooding through his whole body.

Once normal sized again, Alex walked back into the kitchen feeling rather hungry after his spider catastrophe.

'Where have you been? You weren't in your bed this morning!' Alex's mum asked, sounding quite concerned.

'Oh, just checking on the garden, Mum,' Alex replied innocently.

From that day on Alex never squashed another spider. He used to squash spiders: now he's set up the Alexander Thomas Spider Sanctuary! Now whenever you see a spider, resist the urge to squash it, because you never know what might happen to you!

Gemma Daubeney, age 9
Jersey College for Girls Preparatory School,
Jersey

'From now on there are no more school rules,' my teacher announced. 'Stars will be awarded for mischief.'
I was going to be top of the class...

Matt and Dave

Give them back!

by Orla Heatley

**'From now on there are no more school rules,'
my teacher announced. 'Stars will be awarded
for mischief.'**

I was going to be top of the class...

'What happens when we get stars?' Ollie
asked.

'OK fine,' Mr Rover said. 'There are no stars.
I went a bit overboard.' He turned around and
wrote *The One Rule* on the whiteboard. Silence
engulfed the classroom. He continued to write:
*Everyone must come to the school, and not leave the
school grounds between the time of 9am and 3pm,
except on Tuesday, when P.E. keeps the older students
here until 4.15.*

He stopped and looked at us. 'Do you
understand?'

I gulped. No one said anything.

Mr Rover smiled. 'Good.'

'Wait!' I called. 'I don't get it. We can just do
anything we want?'

'Absolutely,' Mr Rover nodded. 'Other than
leave the school grounds, you can do anything
you want. I will just continue with the lessons. If

you want to learn, you can. If not, well, that's OK too.'

The class was in shock. I was anyway. Why would they want to take away the rules? I was curious, but said nothing else, in fear of looking stupid in front of everyone.

'But sir!' Angie protested. 'Why would you do that? Surely the school can't function without rules?'

'I might as well explain,' Mr Rover said. He strolled calmly over to his desk and sat on it. On the desk, not the chair, which was highly unlike him. 'Who, in this room, has broken a school rule since they came here?'

I raised my hand. Heaven knew I was telling the truth. I was no angel. It wasn't that I was bad, I just wasn't particularly good. I glanced around at the 24 other people in the classroom. I saw 24 hands high in the air.

'See?' Mr Rover continued. 'Matt…' at this point he gestured at Matt, sitting in the front row of seats. 'Yesterday, from the staffroom window, I saw you running across the road to get your football. Are you allowed to go across the road without permission?'

Matt went red. Mr Rover stood up and walked over to Isabel. 'You've been wearing make-up in school for quite a while now… last time I checked you're not allowed.'

Rover was right. Isabel's cheeks were pink with blush, her eyes covered in mascara, eyeliner and eyeshadow. Her lips were blood red from her bold lipstick, and her skin was covered in foundation. Her fingernails were painted a bold pink.

'And Jake!' He walked over to the class bully, who knew nothing and was always just seeking attention. 'Well…' Rover paused, unsure of what to say. 'Jake. That's all I need to say.'

The class sniggered. Jake looked around, bewildered, wondering what everyone was laughing at.

'What's your point?' I heard someone at the back shout.

'My point?' Mr Rover raised his eyebrows, as if this was an amusing joke. 'No one's obeying the rules… so yeah, what's the point?'

'What, of having rules?' Ollie asked loudly.

Rover breathed out heavily. 'Yes.'

The class went utterly silent. I thought about what my teacher had just explained. He was looking around now, staring at us all. He looked amused. He was enjoying this. All I wanted to know was why would they remove the rules in the first place? It was cool, but weird.

Suddenly, Mr Rover burst out with, 'All right! History books out please! We're on page 53. Chapter six. The Aztecs.'

Nobody moved. Mr Rover sat in his chair and began reading. '*Before the Europeans invaded, Aztecs were the inhabitants of Mexico and small areas of the Americas…*'

'Sir,' I enquired, 'may I go to the bathroom?'

He shrugged. 'Whatever.' His eyes returned to the history book.

Two weeks later

'Uh!' I yelled. 'Be quiet will you?' I pointed at Jake, Patrick, Gerry and Sam.

They were storming around the classroom, chanting, 'We will, we will, *rock you!*'

It was doing my head in. After two weeks, I was sick. Sick of having nothing to do. Sick of no one being quiet or reasonable. Sick of the immature people going around like they owned the place. I had even resorted to going back to class! And trying to learn. *Trying* to learn. I needed a break.

I had told my mum, dad, older brother. None of them took me seriously. They would just laugh at me. 'No rules!' they would repeat, chuckling. 'Stop playing!'

Well, I was sick of it. Although I wouldn't admit it to my friends, I wanted the rules back. And now, I was going to get them. I stormed out of the room when Jake's gang began the next verse of '*We Will Rock You!*'

Where did I go? To the principal.

'Mr Daniels!' I bellowed. 'Bring back the rules! I hate this! Why did you get rid of them?'

The principal looked up. He had been writing on a small sheet of paper. He gestured at the chair in front of him. 'Sit.' I did as he said.

'You are the…' he glanced at the paper, 'twenty-sixth person to say something along those lines.' He grinned.

'What's that supposed to mean?' I groaned.

'Don't you understand?' he explained. 'Twenty-five other people have complained about our abolishment of our rules. They want them back. And so do you. This is exactly what we wanted.' He chuckled. 'Can you grasp what I'm saying? This was all-'

'A test!' I exclaimed. 'You *knew* this would happen! But… why?'

Mr Daniels leaned back in his chair, relaxed. 'So many children are complaining and moaning and groaning about the rules, so we got rid of them. And now? They want them back!'

'I get it! You wanted everyone to admit the rules were there for a reason, and this was the only way.'

He nodded, smiling from ear to ear now. He wrote something on the end of his sheet of paper, then handed it to me.

I quickly counted the names. There were 26, with my name at the end.

'When are you bringing the rules back?' I couldn't keep the smile off my face. Mr Daniels, who I often underestimated, was smarter than he looked.

'Another two weeks, I'd say. We hope to have *most* of the school asking for them back. Can you wait that long?'

'Suppose,' I replied. 'Can I tell anyone?'

'I'd prefer if you didn't,' he said seriously. I nodded, understanding. I stood up to leave.

'And…' Daniels added quickly, smiling some more. 'Have fun while you still can, won't you?'

I laughed and nodded again. 'Thanks.'

Epilogue

Sixteen days later, Mr Daniels announced to the school what he had told me. Apparently, by this time, 83 per cent of the kids in the school had come to him, requesting the rules back. Some, mainly the 17 per cent who hadn't, weren't happy it was all a test. But everyone had a bit more respect for the rules now.

Just a bit, mind.

Orla Heatley, aged 12
Wicklow Montessori, Co.Wicklow, Ireland

Rules Out!

by Emily Brown

**'From now on there are no more school rules,'
my teacher announced. 'Stars will be awarded
for mischief.'**

I was going to be top of the class...

My teacher kept going on and on but I
wasn't paying attention, for two reasons; A – I
was so excited about going outside and getting
into fights and climbing trees for the rest of my
two remaining years at primary school, and B – I
was totally bewildered that our school, meant to
be one of the strictest in the county, was finally
banishing rules! Suddenly, the bell rang and it
startled me so much that I fell off my chair. I was
waiting for the teacher to tell me off for being silly
but she just fell about laughing.

Everyone ran down the hall at break. Mr
Potts was slowly making his way down the stairs,
one step at a time. I thought he was coming to
patrol the hallway but to my surprise, he stopped
to whisper in a little girl's ear. I can have really
big ears when I want! He was telling her to trip
up someone when they scurried past. She giggled
uncertainly as if he was just joking. This was

getting too weird for me so I raced outside.

My best friend Tom bumped into me as I exited the hallway. 'Ben, can you actually believe that there are no rules! I saw some year sixes scribbling on the list of rules in the hall.'

We went and had a look at what would have been called 'vandalism'.

<u>RULES</u>
- ~~Behave~~ - MISBEHAVE!
- ~~Be kind~~ - BE RUDE
- ~~Drink lots of water~~ - DRINK LOTS OF COKE
- ~~No fighting~~ - FIGHT!
- ~~Respect others~~ - DIS-RESPECT OTHERS
- ~~Listen to teachers~~ - IGNORE TEACHERS

'Is that the best they can do? Scribble on pieces of paper?' I enquired.

'Sshhh, one of them is coming!' Tom exclaimed.

I turned my head away from the new list of rules and winced: there in front of me was Carl Hogglesburg, the boy I have dreaded noticing me for a year.

'So, Ben, I hear you've been 'dissing' our masterpiece, very disrespectful,' Carl snarled.

'I do believe that being disrespectful is on *your* list of rules. Sloppy handwriting by the way,' I replied daringly.

'You better shut that mouth of yours, or me and you are going to have a fight,' he warned.

I gulped. I had never been in a scrap with

Carl before, or anyone for that matter. 'You're on!' I squeaked. I had to say yes because I didn't want to sound chicken.

Then Carl lunged at me and punched my face. I hit back, kicking his leg. Then we started taking it in turns hurting each other, it was not my idea of a fight at all.

Through the corner of my eye, I could see old Mr Potts limping towards us. I screamed for help but all Mr Potts yelled was, 'Get him in the leg Carl! Ben, strike at him while he is in pain!'

Then Mrs Prichard came marching over. I thought she was going to yell encouragements too, but she screamed, 'BREAK IT UP! BEN SMITH, CARL HOGGLESBURG, DETENTION! Someone's got to have a little discipline on a day like this.'

I don't want to talk about what happened in detention. All I am saying is that Carl was throwing paper balls at my head so I spat my bubble gum out on his head, but unfortunately, Mrs Prichard saw me through her misty spectacles and beady red eyes. So I have detention tomorrow as well.

The next day I thought I had better catch up on no rules, so I spat at Mrs Prichard. She didn't laugh this time, she belted at the top of her voice: 'BEN SMITH! THAT'S IT! I'VE HAD ENOUGH OF YOUR LUDICROUS BEHAVIOUR! DOUBLE DETENTION FOR THE REST OF THE WEEK!'

'No,' I bawled, 'I don't have to seeing as it's

no rules. I don't see why I had to go yesterday either.'

'That was completely up to you. But you will still have to go to these detentions,' she replied, calmly. 'And what's all this nonsense about no rules today?'

'Oh, I...' I began.

'Excuses, excuses, I have had it up to the limit with you, stand outside my classroom, now.'

After school, Tom phoned me up and gave me this long, long lecture about how rude I was to Mrs Prichard and that I shouldn't have pretended that it was still No Rules day.

'Hang on, No Rules *day?* I thought it was forever!' I interrupted.

'Well then, you should have listened to Mrs Prichard then, it serves you right!'

Tom was right, it did serve me right.

Emily Brown, aged 10
Hunloke Park Primary School, Derbyshire

Until my last birthday,
I used to think Aunt
Mary was a kind
person.

Stewart Ross

Illustration by Imogen Ross Smith and Alexandra Stanford, Age 8, Ipswich High Junior School.

A Brilliant Birthday Present

by Sam Wheeler

Until my last birthday, I used to think Aunt Mary was a kind person. On my last birthday I was nine. Aunt Mary gave me a shoebox wrapped in horrible, dusty brown paper.

'I've been saving it,' she had said.

I unwrapped the paper and opened the equally dirty box; inside lay the remains of a small toy plane. It was made out of no material I could recognise. The wings had been torn off, the tail was snapped – really it was of no use at all.

'Uhhhhh – thanks!' I lied.

I closed the box, took it up to my room and did not touch it again, thinking Aunt Mary was making a joke out of my birthday. Eventually, Mum took it down out of my room and into the garage...

One sunny Saturday morning, I was looking around the garage for my football, when I noticed an old, dusty shoebox, just lying there. Curious, I picked it up and opened the lid. It was my so-called plane. I took two halves of a wing out and pushed them together. They stuck. I tipped out the seriously broken toy and started sticking the pieces together. I kept at it for an hour or so until it was fixed; then looked at it. Well, at least it was whole, but Aunt Mary hadn't left any instructions, had she?!

'Lunch!' called Mum from the kitchen, so I put the toy down and hurried off, quickly forgetting about it.

The next day, Sunday, was another scorcher. I got up and dressed, had breakfast, then went outside. It was then that I remembered my toy plane.

I know, I'll play with that, I thought, *if it doesn't break!* I opened the garage door and gasped in surprise! Standing in front of me was a full-size, small, double-seater open aircraft. It looked exactly like the one I had made yesterday, except much bigger!

There was a note stuck to the nose.

Dear Sam, I know you like aeroplanes, so I decided to give you this. I hope you find out how to fly it; we don't want any accidents do we?!
Love Aunt Mary.

I gazed in awe at the magnificent machine. It was blue with white stripes on the large double wings. There were two large round holes, one behind the other, where the seats were. I examined it and found a flying kit in the back seat. It contained a navy blue jacket, a hat, goggles and brown gloves.

I climbed inside the cockpit having put on

the flying kit. I slapped my hand on the 'Ignite Engines' button and the propeller whirred loudly into life. The plane moved out of the garage and onto the road. Instinctively I eased the joystick back and the plane soared up into the air.

I knew how to fly a plane without being taught! I put its nose down and dived from 400ft to 100ft. Suddenly I had an idea and pulling the joystick back, headed off towards Aunt Mary's house. Zooming back down, I landed in the field just behind Aunt Mary's bungalow. She was gardening, so saw me over the fence.

'Hi!' I called.

Aunt Mary called back. 'So you found out how to work it then?'

'Yes – thank you so much!' I replied.

'My granddad was a very clever RAF officer and he made it. As you know, I don't have any children of my own, so I decided to give it to you.'

'Do you want a ride?' I asked her.

'Gosh no, I hate flying; that's why I didn't keep it for myself!' Aunt Mary chuckled.

'Is there anything I need to know about it?' I asked.

'Well, it's called an F.E. It was one of the planes used in World War One, but your great-granddad, shall we say, altered it slightly,' Aunt Mary said, smiling.

Having said goodbye, I clambered back into the plane and started the engine. I flew just below the clouds, following the road back a few miles to my house, before circling and landing again. I taxied down the road and then back into the garage.

I leapt out and placed the flying kit back where I had found it, then pressed a large red button at the top of the dashboard labelled 'Shrink/Grow'. I watched incredulously as the plane shrunk back into a toy before my eyes. I ran up to my room with the now toy plane and started playing with it. Mum came into the room: 'What are you doing?' she queried.

'Playing!' I responded.

'With what?'

'Oh – just a toy plane I fixed.'

Did I mention that Aunt Mary is the kindest person in the world?! I wonder what I'll get on my next birthday!

Sam Wheeler, age 9
Woodstone Community Primary School,
Leicestershire

The Poisoned Juice

by Emma Kerslake

Until my last birthday I used to think Aunt Mary was a kind person. That was until I found out who she really was. This is how it started –

It was the day before my birthday and I was outside playing on the swing when she suddenly burst out screaming with fright.

'What's wrong, Aunty?' I said sweetly, gazing at her.

'Nothing!' she sharply said. 'Go to bed.'

The next day I woke up feeling very happy, as it was my birthday. I came downstairs and made myself a piece of toast and a cup of orange juice. I was just about to take it upstairs when my aunty crept up behind me.

'You go back to bed,' she grinned, 'I'll make your breakfast.'

So upstairs I went but soon stopped in my tracks, for downstairs I heard my aunty muttering some strange words. I peered down the stairs and saw her pouring some rather strange green powder into my orange juice. I felt an icy shiver tremble down my back.

'Your breakfast is ready,' she grinned, her

eyes glowing. 'And make sure you drink up <u>ALL</u> of your orange juice.'

I stumbled back upstairs with the orange juice in my hand. What was my aunty doing? Was the green powder harmful?

I sat on my bed and started to think. At that very moment my aunty's black cat, Scratcher, leapt on me growling and whining. A thought suddenly dawned on me – 'Here you are Scratcher,' I said, pouring the orange juice into his little saucer, 'drink up.' He then began slurping it up and a moment later he started screeching and howling. His tail was slowly shrinking and the same was happening to his head. Within seconds there was nothing left of Scratcher.

I took a few steps back, my mind racing. What was I going to do? My heart suddenly pounded – witches have black cats and broomsticks! I knew my aunty had Scratcher who was a black cat, and I always saw her sweeping the house with a wooden broomstick. *She must be a witch*, I thought.

I ran down the stairs screaming at the top of my lungs. I saw my aunty behind me, looking puzzled.

'Drink up your orange juice!' she yelled, trying to be heard over my loud screaming.

I stopped and looked at her. 'You tried to poison me,' I cried, 'how could you do such a thing?'

She stopped shouting and glared back at me.

'You would not understand,' she cackled, her eyes flashing. 'But would you like to have one more birthday surprise?'

I looked around, but there was no escape.

She then started to pull off the skin on her face. Underneath the skin her face was covered in fat, black, juicy maggots. I screamed again, and fainted.

The next thing I knew, I was in bed asleep, with my aunty shaking me. 'Wake up Billy, it's your birthday!' She started singing Happy Birthday to me.

I thought that the green powder was just a dream. She handed me a cup of orange juice.

'Drink up, Billy,' she smiled, flashing her shiny white teeth.

It was then that I noticed a fat black maggot crawling from behind her ear. She turned around and I saw one in her hair. I stared at her, fixated. They were just like the ones in my dream.

I slowly lifted up the cup to see it was a sort of greeny-orangey colour. I looked up at her and screamed…

Emma Kerslake, age 10
Bell Farm School, Surrey

I will never forget the day I met the cuckoo.

Andy Stanton

Maggie's Tale
by Ria Burke

I will never forget the day I met the cuckoo. I
mean, I had heard about him from Granny and
all, God bless her soul, but I had never really
believed it fully. Granny told us about this
possessed creature, but to be honest, it didn't
sound very believable and more like another
old-timer's legend.

My Great-Granny Maggie passed away
due to old age two months ago. She was born
and bred in Galway and she was a very spiritual
person who believed in all those old Irish legends
that you read in primary-school history books.
A few weeks before she left us she told my twin
brother and sister, Alan and Anna, and me the
old tale of an enchanted cuckoo who rests in the
trees of dark forests and only reveals itself at
the scenes of tragedies about to happen, flying
in circles through the air, before disappearing.
However, my siblings and I just laughed at this
and assumed it was our granny's old age talking.

But a couple of days ago I was walking home
after a long, hard day in school when I had my
first encounter with this mystical creature. It was

just after leaving my best friend Aurelia at her gate when it happened. I was sprinting down the lane to my house, past the same old farms and fields that I saw every day, but as I came to the old woods between my house and the road I heard a strange, somewhat enticing 'cuckoo' noise coming from the old horse chestnut tree by the river. Unable to stop myself I ran towards the noise. A large cuckoo was perched on the tree's highest branch. Suddenly, it took flight and swooped upwards and started flying in circles above the river. I thought it strange but walked on home.

The following morning I was shocked when I read the headlines on the front of the newspaper. 'BOY DROWNS IN WESTBRIDGE WOODS RIVER' was plastered across the front page. Reading on I found that he had drowned directly under the spot where the cuckoo had been circling in the air! I carefully avoided the path through the woods to school that day. *This couldn't be a coincidence*, I thought. Things like this just don't happen.

That was when things started to get really weird. I kept seeing the cuckoo in news reports and in photos of disaster scenes. I tried my utmost to ignore it but I just couldn't. If I told anyone I knew I would be branded a mad person, just like we'd thought Maggie was a little bit crazy.

But one day I just couldn't take it anymore. I decided to confront the creature in its home in the woods.

It was a frosty Sunday morning. I got dressed and headed for the woods. I spotted him by the river. Like a lunatic I charged up to him and started shouting at him.

'What are you doing? Why is this happening to me?' I screamed.

Then in the wind, an old yellowed piece of paper blew up into my face. As I caught it in my hands, old-style handwriting started to appear on it.

'*Long ago in ancient Ireland, Saoirse was the daughter of the High King of Connaught. She was known as 'caomhnóir na gcuach' – guardian of the cuckoos, on account of her love for these birds. One night she was away from home and on returning the following morning she learned that her entire family had been murdered by a neighbouring clan*,' the page read.

'*Grief stricken, she cried out, 'If only I had been warned!' From that day forward, my ancestors, Saoirse's cuckoos, vowed to try to warn people of tragedies in Saoirse's memory...*'

I sat there on the riverbank for at least three hours communicating with the cuckoo, getting my replies on the tattered sheet. It was all made clear in time. The cuckoo was a member of a family of cuckoos who had all, in their time, done the same as he was doing now.

Then the cuckoo explained that it was time for him to leave and use his talents elsewhere. He apologised for any distress caused, and explained he only wanted to warn and help people.

As he took flight and disappeared across the horizon it came into my mind that maybe I had been a bit too sceptical about a lot of things I was told. No doubt I had learned a valuable lesson. As my great-granny had often said, '*Ní mar a síltear a bítear*' – things are not always as they seem.

Ria Burke, age 11
Bunscoil na Toirbhirte, Mitchelstown, Co. Cork.

Cuckoo Magic

by Emily James

I will never forget the day I met the cuckoo. He had a broken wing and a dirty tail. He was poking out of a small, dusty, red, wooden house.

It was the first time I had been into our attic. I was with my mother, getting down the Christmas decorations for the start of December.

'What is that?' I asked.

'It used to be a cuckoo clock,' she said. 'It's old and broken now. We should throw it away really.'

'Can I have it?' I asked.

At first Mum said no but I promised to clean it.

'Pleeeease Mum,' I begged, and at last she said yes.

That day Dad helped me fix the cuckoo's wing and clean the clock. I even found a little bit of red paint for it. It was still broken and didn't work but I thought it was lovely. I put it on a shelf by my bed.

That night a very strange thing happened. I woke up and heard a faint noise like the wind blowing through the trees. Then the noise said, 'Cuckoo. Hello.'

I turned on my little light and can you imagine how startled I was when I saw the little cuckoo from the clock nod his head and say, 'Cuckoo. Hello. My name's Woody. What's yours?'

I rubbed my eyes. I thought I was dreaming. 'Emily,' I said.

Then Woody, the cuckoo, began to talk to me. He told me he had been very lonely and sad stuck in the gloomy attic and dreamed of being released into the wild. He was so sad that I wanted to help him but I didn't know how.

The next morning Woody was silent and still. I wondered if it had all been a dream. But on the next night the same thing happened and on the next nights too. Woody would talk to me and tell me his dreams and I told him my secrets. We were good friends. He liked to hear stories about the other birds, how they flew and made their nests. He really liked the story of how cuckoos come and tell us that it is Spring.

One night I carried him to the window so that he could see the stars and the Christmas lights twinkling. But it made him want to be a real bird even more. I knew that I had to try to help him. But how?

Then when I was writing my letter to Father Christmas an idea popped into my mind. I wrote:

Dear Santa,

I wish for Christmas that my little wooden cuckoo can be made real. Love Emily

I crossed my fingers tightly when I sent it.

That night I told Woody about the letter and he was very excited. He asked me about Father Christmas. I told him that Santa was the most magical person in the whole world and I was sure he would make Woody's dream come true.

Finally, Christmas Eve arrived. I was nervous and excited and I thought I would stay awake easily but I did fall asleep. I woke up and heard a faint noise like tiny bells. I turned on my little light and saw Father Christmas in his big red coat tiptoeing out of my room.

'Ho, ho, ho,' he whispered. 'Merry Christmas Emily.'

'Merry Christmas Santa,' I said. 'Did my wish come true?'

'Look and see,' Santa smiled.

I looked at my cuckoo clock. Woody had disappeared. When I turned back Santa had gone too. I hadn't said goodbye.

My mum and dad were surprised that I was a bit quiet on Christmas Day and Boxing Day and the rest of the holiday. Santa had left me other lovely presents but nothing was as nice as Woody. I was happy that my wish had come true but I was sad that I would never see my little friend again.

Then another very strange thing happened. I was sitting on my garden swing one day in March when I heard a noise behind me.

'Cuckoo!' it said loudly.

I looked up and saw a large bird sitting on the hedge. It nodded its head. 'Cuckoo!' it said again. 'And thank you, friend Emily.'

'Hello Woody,' I said. 'Is it Spring?'

Emily James, age 7
Gilwern Junior and Infants School,
Abergavenny

DOODLES AND IDEAS
for more stories

Secret Notes

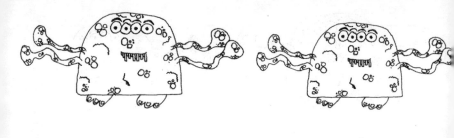

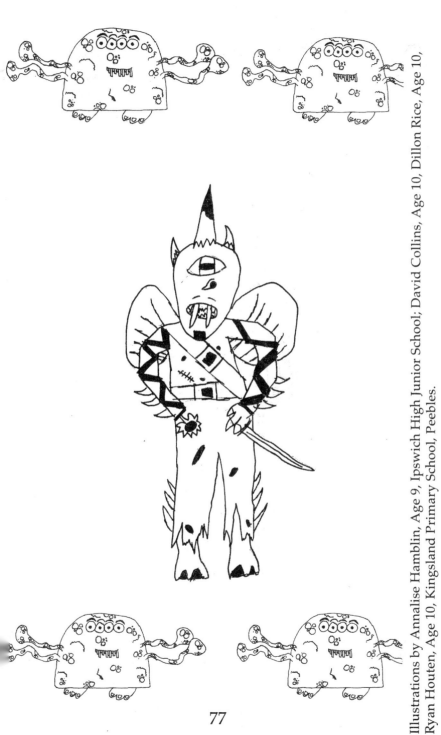

Illustrations by Annalise Hamblin, Age 9, Ipswich High Junior School; David Collins, Age 10, Dillon Rice, Age 10, Ryan Houten, Age 10, Kingsland Primary School, Peebles.